This book belongs to

....

Copyright © 2013

make believe ideas ltd

The Wilderness, Berkhamsted, Hertfordshire, HP4 2AZ.

www.makebelieveideas.com

Written by Tim Bugbird.
Illustrated by Lara Ede.
Designed by Annie Simpson and Sarah Vince.

Annie the Apple Pie Fairy

Tim Bugbird · Lara Ede

make believe ideas

Once in a wood, by a **bubbling** brook,
up high in an old apple tree,
lived a fairy named Annie, a famous cook,
who baked **apple pies** on TV!

She had her own show
for years and years,
with her best friends,
Pip and Cora.

Every show ended with
whoops and **cheers** –
the fairies simply **adored** her!

All Annie's pies were made with **care**,
simply, and with **nothing** wasted.

Whether with currants, or berries and pears,
they were the best you've ever tasted!

Then one day the TV screens
turned a little glary.
In a blaze of colour, a new face appeared:

Sondra the Strudel Fairy!

Sondra's style was fancy –
her pies were never plain.
The fairies switched to Sondra's show,
time and time again!

Pip declared, "Chef Sondra

will beat us if we let her.

So we must do what Sondra does.

But do it much, much better!"

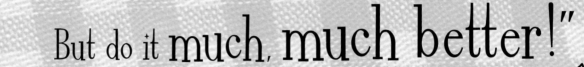

"Sondra **thinks** that she's the **tops**,"
said Cora with a frown.
"We'll have to pull out **all the stops**
to **win** back your **baking crown!**"

And so, between the TV chefs, there arose a competition: to make **fancy bakes** and be **the best** became each fairy's **mission.**

Every pie the rivals made was
fab-ul-ous-ly fashioned,
with **toppings**
and **twirls**
so high they swayed –
decoration was
never rationed!

fancy bakes

Inside Annie's and Sondra's **homes,** the sound you always heard was the **clatter** and **clunk** of gadgets, which became ever more **absurd!**

They had machines for cutting, slicing, peeling, dicing, flaking, shaking, beating and breaking, rolling, moulding, chopping, folding, whipping, mixing, brushing and fixing!

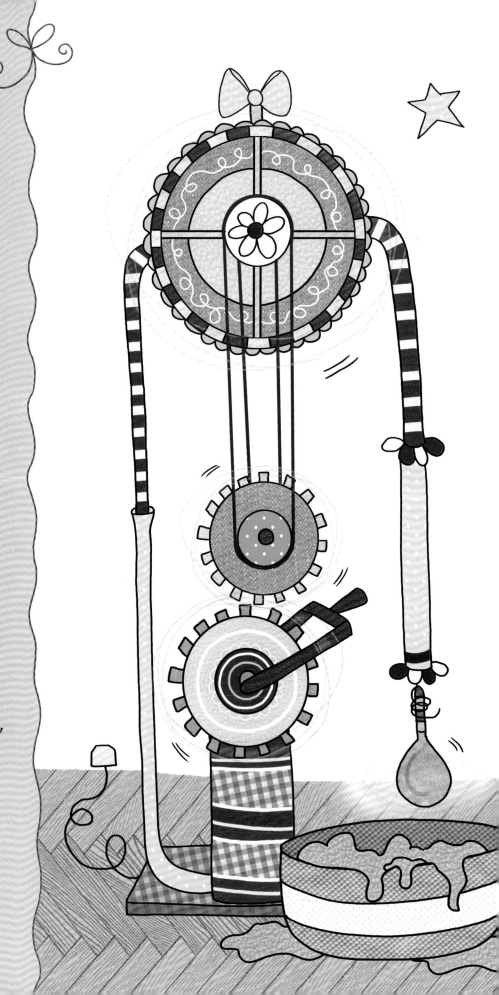

Soon **every** fairy across the land was following **Sondra's** trend.
Bigger, better, never bland – wherever would it **end?**

The machines made every kind of thing, in every **shape** and **size**.

But **nobody** seemed to notice – not one made **apple pies**.

But still the gadgets **pinged** and **popped**, with **whirs** and **purrs** and **clangs**, until the night when everything **stopped**, with a **flash** and a deafening . . .

The fairies had a big surprise —
their power had totally blown!

Feeling scared, they took to the skies,
and flocked to Annie's tree home.

back soon

Annie's house

Pip found **candles** to light the scene
and **slippers** to warm their feet,
but with **nothing** to power
their cooking machines,
what would the **poor**
fairies **eat**?

Candles

Cora **peered** inside the pantry.
Annie joined her in **despair**.
As far as either one could **see**,
there was next to **nothing** there!
Just **apples** . . .
and **butter** . . .
and **sugar** . . .
and **flour**.

Annie **sighed** and said to Sondra,
"I think things got out of hand.
We **forgot** what **matters** in the end,
we just **didn't** understand."

"Now I know what we should do:
we must bake an apple pie.
We'll add a spoonful of loving –
the ingredient money can't buy."

The **pie** was made the **old-fashioned** way,
tasting **sweet**, just as it should.

Sondra said: "Let's not compete,"
and apple pie was back for good!

Annie and Sondra worked together and saw their friendship grow

as they starred with Pip and Cora on their brand-new TV show!